Weekly Reader Children's Book Club presents

Just the Thing for Geraldine

by Ellen Conford

Illustrated by John Larrecq

LITTLE, BROWN AND COMPANY

Boston   Toronto

FIRST EDITION

T 09/74

Library of Congress Cataloging in Publication Data

Conford, Ellen.
   Just the thing for Geraldine.

   SUMMARY: After making her try ballet, weaving, and
sculpture lessons, Geraldine's possum family finally
lets her do what she enjoys most--juggling.
   I. Larrecq, John M., illus. II. Title.
PZ7.C7593Ju   [E]   74-7193
ISBN 0-316-15304-4

Published simultaneously in Canada
by Little, Brown & Company (Canada) Limited

PRINTED IN THE UNITED STATES OF AMERICA

Weekly Reader Children's Book Club Edition

THERE WAS NOTHING Geraldine liked
better than hanging by her tail from the
branch of a tree and juggling a few acorns.

But her parents told her there was more to
life than juggling, so every week she went to
Mademoiselle La Fay's School of the Dance
to learn ballet.

"It will help you to be graceful," said her
mother.

"It will help you to be ladylike," said her
father.

"It will help you keep physically fit," said
her brother Randolph.

"Nothing could help her," whispered her
brother Eugene.

One day Geraldine came home from ballet school very excited.

"Everybody come look!" she shouted. "Come look at what I can do!"

"What is it?" asked her mother.

"We learned the Dance of the Purple Swan," Geraldine said.

"That's wonderful!" said her mother.

"A whole dance!" exclaimed her father. "And you haven't even been going to dancing school very long."

"Swans aren't purple," said Eugene.

"Now, watch me," Geraldine ordered. "Are you looking?"

"We're looking," said her mother.

Geraldine smoothed down her tutu, which her mother had made for her out of leaves, and gracefully raised her forepaws over her head.

"Dee, da da da da dee ta dum," she hummed, and ran lightly, on tiptoe, around the trunk of the tree.

"Oh, how beautiful," sighed her mother.

"Encore, encore!" clapped her father.

"That's pretty good, Geraldine," said Randolph.

"Can we go play now?" asked Eugene.

"Dee, da da da da ta dum," Geraldine hummed, and began to dance faster around the tree.

But one of the big roots of the tree was sticking up from the ground and Geraldine didn't see it.

"Ow!" yelled Geraldine, as she tripped over the root and sprawled on the ground.

"Did you hurt yourself?" asked her mother worriedly.

"No," Geraldine sniffled, and ran up the
tree before Randolph and Eugene could see
her tears. She hung upside down by her tail,
her leafy ballet skirt covering her face.

"I see you, Randolph," she said angrily.
"You think I can't see you, but I can. You'd
better stop laughing."

Randolph covered his mouth with his paw.

"I'm not laughing," he said, trying to sound
serious.

"Is it all right if *I* laugh?" asked Eugene.

"There is nothing to laugh at," their father
said sternly.

"Geraldine just tripped," their mother said.
"It could happen to anyone."

"Especially Geraldine," whispered Eugene
to Randolph.

"I heard you, Eugene!" Geraldine shouted. "You think I can't hear you, but I can!" She pulled herself back up on the branch and straightened her tutu. "I'd like to see you do the Dance of the Purple Swan."

"Swans aren't purple," said Eugene. "Swans are white."

Randolph and Eugene went back to their game. Geraldine took off her ballet skirt. She looked at it thoughtfully as she folded it and put it away.

The following week, when Geraldine came home from ballet school, her mother and father were waiting for her.

"Well, what did you learn at dancing school today?" her mother asked eagerly.

"I learned," said Geraldine unhappily, "that I am not a very good dancer."

"Nonsense!" said her father. "You dance beautifully. And you haven't even been going to dancing school very long."

"And I don't think I'll be going much longer," said Geraldine.

"Oh, of course you will," said her mother. "You'll see, you'll be a graceful dancer in no time."

Geraldine shook her head.

"No I won't," she said. "I cannot do pliés and arabesques, and when we're supposed to dance on our toes my toes curl up and I fall down. I am just not cut out for ballet."

"But I thought you liked ballet school," said her mother.

"I like juggling better," said Geraldine.

"But don't you want to learn to be graceful?" asked her father.

"No," said Geraldine, swinging back and forth by her tail from the branch of the tree and juggling some pebbles. "Not really."

"Oh," said her mother.

After Geraldine stopped going to ballet school, her mother enrolled her in Mrs. Winkelman's Weaving Class.

"Weaving?" said Geraldine. "I don't think I—"

"You'll really like weaving," her mother promised brightly. "You can learn how to make little baskets and rugs and place mats, and when you grow up and have a family of your own you can make all kinds of things for them."

Geraldine did not do well in weaving class.

So, her mother signed her up for a class at Schuyler's School of Sculpture.

"I'm sure you have artistic talent," said her mother.

"Sculpture school is just the thing for you, Geraldine," agreed her father.

"I don't know," said Geraldine doubtfully, as she flipped three blackberries in the air and balanced a twig on the end of her nose.

"Oh, you'll see," said her mother. "You'll make bowls and pitchers and artistic statues. Sculpture school will be lots of fun."

Every week Geraldine went to Schuyler's School of Sculpture, and every week her parents asked, "How do you like sculpture school?"

And every week Geraldine shrugged and said, "It's okay, I guess."

One day Geraldine came home from class carrying a big pile of something wrapped in wet leaves.

"What's that?" asked Randolph.

"That's clay," said Geraldine.

"What's it for?" asked Eugene curiously.

"We have to make a sculpture of someone," Geraldine said.

"Oh, boy!" cried Eugene, jumping up and standing very straight and flexing his muscles. "Do me, Geraldine, do me!"

"We just have to do the head," Geraldine said.

"Oh," said Eugene, disappointed. "Well," he brightened a minute later, "do my head." He turned his head sideways so Geraldine could see his profile. "I have a nice head. Please, Geraldine?"

"You have to sit very still," Geraldine warned. "You can't move around or wiggle or anything."

"I won't," promised Eugene. "I won't even blink."

Geraldine sat Eugene down in front of her and turned his head sideways. She unwrapped the mound of clay and put it on a tree stump. Randolph sat down next to her.

"Don't sit there and watch me!" Geraldine snapped. "How do you expect me to concentrate when you're staring at me like that?"

"You're very touchy," said Randolph. "Why are you in such a bad mood?"

"I'm not in a bad mood!" yelled Geraldine. "Now, go away and leave me alone!"

Randolph went off to play ball and Geraldine began to work on her sculpture.

After a while, Eugene began to squirm.

"Is it finished yet, Geraldine?" he asked.

"No," said Geraldine.

"My nose itches," complained Eugene.

"Sit still and be quiet!" Geraldine ordered.

Geraldine molded the clay, squeezing it, poking it, and muttering to herself while she worked.

"What are you saying, Geraldine?" Eugene asked. "I can't hear you."

"I'm saying 'stupid clay!'" Geraldine snapped. "Now will you be still? How can I sculpt you if you keep wriggling around?"

"I can't help it," Eugene whined. "I'm getting tired. My neck hurts. And I think I have to sneeze."

"Be quiet. And I'm doing your mouth now, so please keep it shut."

Eugene sighed. Geraldine went on molding and muttering.

Finally she said, "There. It's done. I think."

"Oh, good!" said Eugene, jumping up and stretching. "I feel stiff all over. Let's see it."

But Geraldine was covering her sculpture with the wet leaves.

"Let me see it," Eugene said. "Why are you covering it up? I want to see my head."

He ran over to the tree stump and began pulling off the leaves.

"Stop it!" yelled Geraldine, swatting at him. "You stop that, Eugene! I don't want you to look at it. I don't want *anybody* to look at it."

"I won't hurt it," Eugene said, yanking off the leaves. "I want to see it."

Randolph and their mother and father came running when they heard Eugene and Geraldine.

"What's going on?" asked their father.

"Why are you two screaming like this?" asked their mother.

"*What* is *that?*" Randolph asked, pointing toward the tree stump.

Eugene had pulled all the leaves off Geraldine's sculpture and was backing away from the tree stump, shaking his head in fury.

"That is *not me!*" he howled. "I don't look like that!"

"Well, if you didn't move around so much —" Geraldine shouted.

"Is *that* supposed to be *Eugene?*" Randolph asked.

"It's . . . it's very interesting," their father said weakly.

"It is not interesting!" shrieked Eugene. "It's a bunch of lumps! I don't look like a bunch of lumps!"

Geraldine sighed, and began to cover up her sculpture with leaves again. When she finished covering it all up, she climbed the tree and hung by her tail, swinging gently back and forth as she juggled some pine cones.

A little while later Randolph and Eugene came up the tree and sat down next to Geraldine.

"You sure are a good juggler, Geraldine," said Randolph kindly.

"Thank you," Geraldine murmured.

Randolph gave Eugene a poke in the ribs.

"Ow! I mean, oh," said Eugene, "I wish I could juggle like you can."

"Do you really?" Geraldine asked.

"You're the best juggler we know. ISN'T THAT RIGHT, EUGENE?" said Randolph, glaring at his brother.

"Yes," Eugene said.

"So we'd like you to teach us how to juggle," Randolph said. "WOULDN'T WE, EUGENE?"

"Yes," Eugene said.

"Oh," said Geraldine, happily, "of course
I'll teach you. It's not too hard, once you get
the hang of it. Now, just watch me and —"

"Geraldine!" her mother called. "I've thought of just the thing for you!"

"What is it?" asked Geraldine.

"Singing lessons!" her mother said excitedly. "How would you like to take singing lessons?"

"No," said Geraldine, juggling her acorns.

"No?" her father asked. "But you'd love singing lessons."

"No," repeated Geraldine. "I wouldn't."

"But, why not, Geraldine?" asked her mother.

"What if I'm not a good singer?" said Geraldine. "I took ballet lessons and found out I wasn't a good dancer. I took weaving lessons, and found out I wasn't a good weaver."

"And you certainly aren't good at sculpting," Eugene added.

"She sure is a good juggler, though," said Randolph. "And nobody ever gave her juggling lessons."

"That's true," their mother said.

"I never thought of that," said their father.

"Neither did I," said Geraldine.

Suddenly, she stopped juggling and jumped up.

"I'll be right back," she said, and ran down the tree.

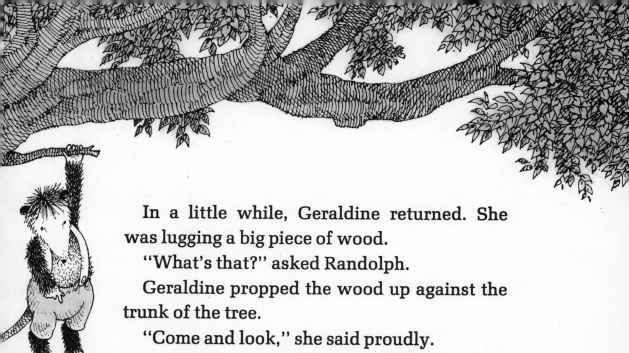

In a little while, Geraldine returned. She was lugging a big piece of wood.

"What's that?" asked Randolph.

Geraldine propped the wood up against the trunk of the tree.

"Come and look," she said proudly.

The possums came down from the tree.

"I made a sign," said Geraldine.

"What kind of a sign?" asked Eugene. "What does it say?"

"Oh, it's beautiful," said their mother.

"Aren't you the clever one!" said their father.

"What does it *say*?" cried Eugene. "Tell me what it says!"

"It says," Randolph told him,

GERALDINE'S
JUGGLING
SCHOOL